ADVENTURES IN FRONTIER AMERICA

Texas Roundup

Life on the Range

by Catherine E. Chambers
illustrated by John Lawn

Troll

Young Juan stubbornly faced his father, Guillermo Carson. They had had this argument many times before. "I am almost a man," said Juan, his voice echoing across the long adobe room. "It is *time* I learned to ride in the roundup and the cattle drive. Otherwise no one will respect me!"

His father sighed. "Juan, we have been over this before. You know your grandmother thinks you are not yet old enough. It would worry her."

Juan stubbornly stuck out his chin. "That's not why, and you know it," he said. "Grandmother doesn't want me to go *ever*. Soon she'll be saying I've gotten too old to learn."

Grandmother Maria had raised Juan and his sister, Graciela, since their mother had died. She was a little old lady with blue-black hair and beautiful dark eyes. They snapped now proudly. "The grandson of Samuel Carson, one of the greatest ranchers in all Texas, should not be part of such common things. A great horseman, yes. But work the range with cowhands! No!"

Father pressed his lips together. He loved his mother. But he disliked the way she looked down on the life of their wonderful *Rancho del Sol*. Juan's eyes, so like his grandmother's, snapped, too.

"The grandson of Samuel Carson should know how to do everything that has to be done on our ranch," said Juan. "How else can I live up to Grandfather's example? Who would take orders from me when I am in charge?"

Grandmother's eyes changed. She nodded slowly. "Perhaps you are right. So I have changed my mind." She looked at Juan's father. "But only the roundup now. We will wait till next year for the cattle drive. Then we'll see."

Juan didn't want to argue about that. He bowed to his grandmother and ran out before she could change her mind. Once out of the house, and into the sun-drenched patio, he let out a yell. "I'm going to work the roundup. Wait till I tell Manuel!"

Manuel Garcia was Juan's best friend, almost the brother he didn't have. No one on the ranch, except Guillermo Carson, was respected more than Manuel's father. He was the ranch boss.

Juan and Manuel had lived on *Rancho del Sol* all their lives. So had their fathers. Grandfather Carson had built the great Spanish-style ranch for his Spanish bride when he brought her from Santa Fe. Once, all of the American Southwest had been owned by Spain. Spanish priests had founded missions in Monterey and San Francisco and Santa Barbara. They built others in the Rio Grande valley around Santa Fe, New Mexico, and in Texas. Spanish towns, called *pueblos*, had been built. All the buildings were made of sun-dried mud bricks called *adobe*. The adobe blocks were a foot and a half long, and the walls of the buildings were very thick with small, high windows. This kept the rooms cool under the blazing sun. Poor settlers had one-room *casas*, or houses, with mud floors and corner fireplaces. The missions and a few rich land-owners owned most of the land. These people lived in houses that had many rooms, even many buildings. The buildings opened onto a center court and were linked by a surrounding adobe wall. The town had a wall around it, too, for defense.

In the country beyond the towns, the rich landowners lived in fort-like houses on vast acres. A landowner's farm was called a *hacienda*. If a landowner raised longhorn cattle instead of farming, his place was called a *rancho*. Many of these Spanish homes were very splendid, filled with wrought iron and silver hinges and door handles. Chairs had seats and backs of fine-tooled leather. Silver and velvet were everywhere.

That was the kind of house Grandmother Maria had grown up in. When American adventurer Samuel Carson fell in love with her, he promised to give her one just as splendid. And he had. He gave up traveling the Santa Fe trade route and settled down to start a ranch. Many Americans did this in the early nineteenth century. They had to become Spanish citizens because the land belonged

8

to Spain, but they still thought of themselves as Americans. Then in 1821, Spain lost all the Southwest territory to Mexico. Then the Carsons were Mexican citizens. In 1836, Grandfather Carson had helped Sam Houston fight in the battle at San Jacinto, which freed Texas from Mexico. And in 1845, Texas had become part of the United States.

"So I'm an American," Juan thought. "Grandmother Maria can't do a thing about it!" He loved *Rancho del Sol* as much as his grandmother and father did. He just wished his grandmother didn't look down on people who didn't live as the Carsons did.

"Juan! Why so long-faced? You lose your battle again?" Manuel galloped up on his dusty mustang and grinned down at him.

Juan grinned back. "No, I won it! I'm going with you, Manuel, on the roundup!"

Twice a year, every year, there was a roundup. The cattle of the Southwest were very different from those back East. They were descended from cattle the *conquistadores* brought from Spain hundreds of years before. These cattle were stringy, narrow-faced, and sometimes vicious. They could take care of themselves, out on the open range, grazing on desert grass. Those early Spanish cattle were called *cimarróns*, meaning "wild ones." They crossbred with American cattle into a whole new breed. "They sure are special," Juan thought admiringly, looking out across the range. They were lean but sturdy, and their horns were magnificent—four, five, sometimes even seven feet across!

While Father and other Texans had been fighting in the War Between the States, the longhorn herds had been left to roam wild. When the soldiers came home, they found their stock had survived and multiplied. Cattle born during the war had never been branded with an owner's name. So the notion rose that unbranded cattle belonged to whoever grabbed them first. But most ranchers and their workers were honest. Spring and fall, they went out to round up their own herds, count heads, and brand the new calves. If a man by accident rounded up his neighbor's cow, he usually branded her calf for him with the neighbor's mark.

All their lives, Juan and his sister, Graciela, had waved good-bye as the ranch cowhands, led by Manuel's father, José Garcia, rode out for the great roundup. The past few years, they hadn't been satisfied to wave. "I'm as good with the lariat as you are," Graciela said stubbornly. "I ride as well. I don't see why I can't go, too."

Juan knew how she felt. Graciela wasn't satisfied to sit home embroidering, wearing the ruffled velvets of a Spanish lady—just as he wasn't satisfied to ride around the

corral in a Spanish gentleman's velvet trousers and silver spurs. That was show-off riding and great fun. But he wanted to gallop across the range, eat from the chuck wagon, and sleep among the sagebrush! Well, this year he would!

Spring roundup was held in May. All the stockmen in that part of Texas met and divided the public range into sections a hundred miles square. Each rancher in a section sent out a group of cowboys called *vaqueros*. With them went a string of pack mules. The camp cook rode in a big chuck wagon that held all his cooking needs. It might be three months before anyone on the roundup saw home again, so the cook was a very important man. The chuck wagon also carried bedrolls and supplies.

The week before the roundup began, all the cowboys were busy getting ready. Horses had to be chosen for the trip. The horses of the Southwest, like the longhorn cattle, were very special. They were offspring of horses brought by the Moors to Spain long ago, and to the New World with the *conquistadores*. They were called *mustangs*, from an old Spanish word meaning "strayed." They were also called *broncos*. *Bronco* was Spanish for "rough" or "rude." Mustangs fit both of those descriptions. As Manuel said, "They don't look like much, but they sure can work. And when you've done a day's work, they've still got enough devil in them to kick your hat off!"

Juan already had his own horse, Chino. Like most of the ranch's herd, he was mostly mustang and part American Standard. That made him taller and faster, but no prettier. Juan thought he was beautiful all the same. Juan also had his own lariat, and he knew how to use it, thanks to Manuel and José Garcia. But he needed to get other things ready for the roundup. He wouldn't have to wear the velvets of an owner's son this time! Instead he had rough denim pants to tuck into his high boots, and leather chaps to protect him in thorn thickets. He had bandannas to keep the dust off his neck, and rough, collarless work shirts. He had a short vest, an old, flat-crowned felt hat, and the silver spurs Grandfather had given him.

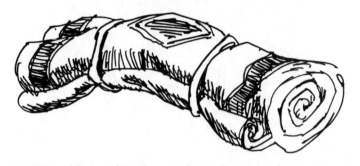

The day before the roundup was to leave, Father called Juan out to the stable. "Now that you will be doing a man's work, it's time you had these," he said, smiling. Juan's jaw dropped. There on the rail was a new saddle, with beautiful designs carved into the leather. The leather covering was stretched over a wooden frame, and the steel horn made a handle for anchoring a rope when needed. There was a new saddle blanket woven in a special pattern. Like all Texas saddles, this one had two bellybands, called *cinches*. Tie-strings held a lariat to the saddle fork and a slicker and blanket to the back of the saddle skirt. They would protect Juan in wet weather.

Best of all, there was a scabbard on the saddle, and in the scabbard was a Colt revolver. Juan drew it out, scarcely daring to breathe. Its silver mountings were engraved *JC*, in a fancy version of the blazing sun that was the brand mark of *Rancho del Sol*. He turned to his father slowly.

"A man on the range needs a gun," Guillermo Carson said. "But a gun is a serious responsibility, and I trust you to use it only when needed."

At last, the great day arrived. Out through the gates of
the ranch the procession streamed. Cowboys, broncos,
mules, and the chuck wagon. José Garcia led the way, his
silver spurs gleaming in the early dawn. Juan, galloping
along beside Manuel, thought he was going to burst with
excitement.

They had many miles to ride before they met the other
roundup parties from their section. At last, Manuel said,
"Look, there!" and Juan squinted against the rising sun.

Far ahead, twenty wagons had gathered by the river. Breakfast fires were brewing coffee for three or four hundred men. The *Rancho del Sol* party joined them. Manuel pulled Juan after him through the crowd. Juan might be a ranch owner's son, but he was new here and very unimportant. There was much work to be done before the roundup could begin. Every man had to be assigned a job. To the boys' delight, José Garcia was again chosen chief of the whole roundup. All the ranchers knew he was the best man for the post. Juan was told to gather kindling for the fires where the branding irons would be heated. He swallowed his disappointment and did as he was told.

Before that first day was over, Juan had more respect than ever for José Garcia and all the cowboys—and their horses! The cattle grazed in small groups all over the district. The cowboys' first job was to herd them into one huge crowd. "How do they know where to look?" Juan said to Manuel. Manuel shouted the answer as he galloped off to help. "Some of our men put rock salt out for them weeks ago. The cattle will be there or by the water."

It would be a few days before branding could begin, so after Juan gathered kindling, he was free to follow Manuel. They saw a *Rancho del Sol* cowhand riding slowly around a bunch of longhorns. As Juan galloped up, the steers lifted their heads and bolted. The cowboy yelled at Juan as if he were any other greenhorn. "Don't you know better than to scare a herd?" After that, Juan ashamedly minded his cattle manners. He stayed back several lengths, watched what Manuel did, and tried to copy.

It sometimes took days, Juan found, for a cowboy to move his small group of cattle back to the big herd. And that big herd grew larger daily. The air was filled with the smell of animals and the sound of cattle bawling. Day and night, the herd was guarded on all sides. Juan learned to sleep on the ground with his tarpaulin beneath his blanket and his saddle for a pillow. At dawn, he ambled to the chuck wagon and sat on the ground to eat a hunk of bread and steak. He drank bitter black coffee out of a tin cup. After a few weeks, he dreamed about soft beds and fresh greens from Grandmother Maria's garden.

The chuck wagon carried flour and corn meal, bacon, lard, and fat-back, and sourdough for biscuits. When beef was needed, a steer was killed. Old Carlos, the cook, soon became one of Juan's best friends. The cowboys teased Carlos with nicknames like "pot wrangler." But Carlos took it all in good spirit and bossed and comforted and advised them all.

After all the cattle in the district had been rounded up, the work of separating each ranch's herd began. Only the best cowboys from each outfit did this. Each cowboy rode slowly among the cattle. He didn't look for the brands, which could be hard to see in a packed herd. Instead he looked for the notch cut in each cow's ear. Each ranch had a notch as distinctive as its brand. When one of José Garcia's cowboys found a *Rancho del Sol* cow, he quietly pointed it out to his pony. Then the pony took over the job. He worked the cow out from the herd by nudging and by getting in her way whenever she tried to turn back. Once a cow was "cut out," another cowboy took over and drove the cow to join the *Rancho del Sol* herd.

For Juan, the most exciting part to watch was the lassoing of the calves. The calves always followed their mothers into the ranch's herd. But then they had to be lassoed and held down for branding.

The Texas lariats were thirty feet long. A cowhand held the coils in his left hand and swung the noose with his right. He had to throw from behind and drop the noose over the calf. Then he flipped the rope to one side while his pony dashed to the other. The rope, lashed to the saddle horn, snapped tight around the calf's legs and pulled them from under him. Then the calf was dragged to the fire. A man put a knee on the calf's back and held on tight. The brander flicked a knife on one ear and brought the branding iron down on a flank. It was over in a minute, with the smell of singed hair and a lot of bawling. Then the calf was free to hightail it back to its mother.

Juan was kept busy gathering fuel. But whenever he had a supply, he sneaked away with Chino and tried some lassoing. He wasn't nearly as good with his lasso as he had thought. He knew the cowboys laughed at him, and he was ashamed. But Chino worked with him like a good

partner. Every day Juan practiced. Every day he got better. He was very proud when, at one noon meal, the *Rancho del Sol* boss said gruffly, "This afternoon you can ride with the cowboys."

One dawn, Manuel rode up to him and clapped his shoulder. "My father says today you and I ride into the next section and round up strays!" That meant they were really trusted—both their horsemanship and their honesty.

At last the roundup was over. It was late July now. The cowboys were bearded and dirty. Dust was ground into their leathery sunburned skins. Juan had slept in his clothes for two months. He was used to Carlos' chuckwagon beans and fiery chili. He even liked the bitter coffee. He knew how much he had learned and how much he still didn't know. He had grown in more ways than he could count.

"Some of them I don't think my grandmother's going to like," he said to Manuel as they rode at last toward the *Rancho del Sol* in the desert sunset.

Manuel grinned. "She wants you to be a man like Samuel Carson, doesn't she?"

Guillermo Carson rode out to meet the procession. He had been out to the roundup many times, staying for days and visiting old friends. Now he was welcoming his ranchers home. He and José Garcia led the procession, with Manuel and Juan proudly beside them. They rattled into the courtyard. Everyone who had stayed home on the ranch was gathered waiting. They clapped and shouted.

The door of the house opened, and Grandmother Maria came out, followed by Graciela. His sister had grown taller, Juan saw. But everybody was watching Maria Carson. She was wearing diamonds in her ears, and her best lace veil on a high carved comb. Her black velvet dress was covered with lace and ruffles, and her black eyes were filled with pride. Juan and Manuel and their fathers swung down and bowed. Juan's father went forward and kissed his mother. Then the old woman came firmly toward Juan. She put one hand on each dirty shoulder. She kissed him formally on each sweaty cheek. Then she hugged him hard, dust and all.

That night, after everybody had cleaned up, there was a fiesta. The next week there was a rodeo. Ranchers and cowhands and their families came from other ranches and stayed for days. Whole steers were roasted over outdoor fires. Carlos made vats of chili. Cowboys showed off their trick riding and had roping contests. The horsemen held races. There were cart races, too, with the thatch-roofed wagons bumping along behind the galloping longhorn oxen. Inside the carts, Graciela and the other girls hung on for dear life.

Everyone wore their best clothes and all their silver. At night, there was dancing, guitar-playing, and singing. Juan was a rancher's son again now and host with his father. But he was happy to see he was still treated as one of the cowhands by the other men. He knew he had "won his spurs."

All that summer and into fall, Juan rode out with the cowboys. He helped with horse-breaking, and went on the fall roundup where beef cattle were herded and calves missed in the spring roundup were branded. This time the men were only out on the range for two weeks. For once, Juan didn't even ask to go on the long drive that took the cows to market.

He knew by now how much more he had to learn. But he worked hard and kept his eyes and ears open. The day he overheard José tell Guillermo Carson that Juan had the makings of a good cowboy, Juan almost burst with pride.

Juan went on the roundup again in spring. This year the rains came more often, and he was glad he had his slicker and tarp. One night when he was standing guard, he saw a cowboy he didn't know sneaking toward the herd. He followed silently as the stranger herded two cows and their calves out from the others. Then Juan crept over to where his horse was tied. A touch brought Chino awake. Juan swung himself up bareback. He didn't even need to speak to Chino, who obeyed Juan's heels and hands. They cantered quietly after the thief.

Not till they were well away from the herd did the stranger prepare to stop. The man was about to get off his horse when Juan suddenly appeared from among the shadows. Pointing his revolver at the stranger, Juan shouted, "Don't move." His heart was pounding, but his voice was steady. His arms were steady, too.

Eyes met eyes. The thief's hand froze, halfway to his holster. Then he dug his heels into his mustang and wheeled, and galloped off across the range.

Juan herded the cattle back to the camp. He didn't say anything about what had happened. He didn't think anybody knew.

Two weeks after the roundup was over, Guillermo Carson called Juan into his office. He was sitting in his great leather chair behind the heavy carved oak desk. Juan loved this room with its hide rugs and trophies and memories of his grandfather. He sat down across from his father, wondering what he was about to say.

For many long seconds, Guillermo Carson looked at Juan across his folded hands. Then he pushed back his chair.

"I want you to go on the long drive this year."

Juan was so excited, he couldn't even speak.

"I am going, too. I haven't been north to Abilene, Kansas, in three years. There are men I must see there, and I want you to meet them. There is talk of bringing the Kansas and Pacific Railroad further west, closer to our cattle. We have to be sure that proper stockyards will be built. Maybe you and I will go by rail from Abilene to Kansas City and inspect the stockyards there."

When Juan found his voice, all he could say was, "Grandmother Maria won't like it."

"Your grandmother understands the time has come. I told her how you drove off that rustler without anyone's coming to harm. You didn't know José Garcia saw it, did you? He told me. He thought I had a right to be proud."

I'm going to be riding out with my father, Juan thought—*riding for weeks north up the Chisholm Trail, then to Elm Spring, Caldwell, Wichita, Abilene.* Names that had just been dots on the map would become real places.

Travel on the long drive could be dangerous. There was danger of a stampede. There was danger of cows panicking at a river crossing. They might meet cattle thieves. Or Indians might ask payment for letting the drive pass through their land. They might find barbed wire stretched across the trail by homesteaders who were settling there. But at the end of the trail, there would be rip-roaring Abilene—and perhaps Kansas City!

No wonder his grandmother hadn't wanted to let him go before, Juan thought, looking back. He *had* been too young. A real greenhorn. But the past two years on the range had taught him so much. Now he, Juan Carson, was ready!

Index

*(Page numbers that appear in **boldface** type refer to illustrations.)*

This edition published 1999 by Troll Communications L.L.C.

Printed in the United States of America.

10   9   8   7   6   5   4   3   2   1

Cover art by Robert F. Goetzl.

Library of Congress Cataloging-in-Publication Data

Chambers, Catherine E.
    Texas roundup.

    (Adventures in frontier America)
    Summary: In nineteenth-century Texas, a young boy
learns a great deal about life on the range when he is
at last allowed to accompany the ranch hands on the
spring roundup.
[1. Ranch life—Fiction.   2. Cattle trade—West
(U.S.)—Fiction.   3. Texas—History—1846-1850—Fiction.
4. Frontier and pioneer life—Texas—Fiction]   I. Lawn,
John, ill.   II. Title.   III. Series: Chambers,
Catherine E. Adventures in frontier America.
PZ7.C3558Te   1984   [Fic]   83-18281
ISBN 0-8167-0047-8 (lib. bdg.)
ISBN 0-8167-5039-4 (pbk.)